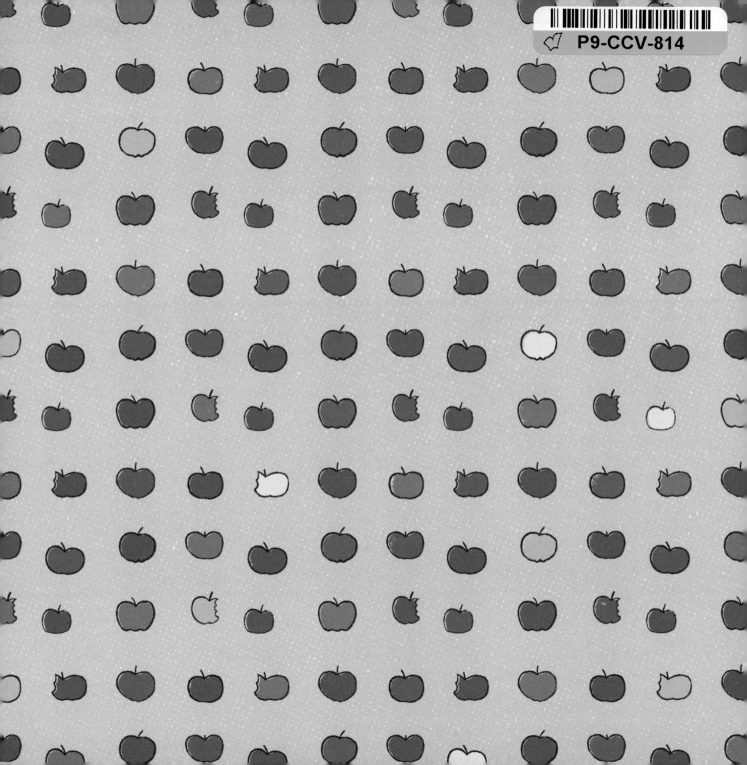

For William Burke Ottiger, who likes apples
—MS

For Sophia
—GP

The art in this book was drawn digitally in Photoshop.

Cataloging-in-Publication Data has been applied for and
may be obtained from the Library of Congress.

ISBN: 978-1-4197-2140-3

Published in 2016 by Abrams Appleseed, an imprint of ABRAMS.

Printed and bound in China
10 9 8 7 6 5 4 3 2 1

For bulk discount inquiries, contact specialsales@abramsbooks.com.

ABRAMS
THE ART OF BOOKS SINCE 1949
115 West 18th Street
New York, NY 10011
www.abramsbooks.com

BY **MARILYN SINGER** ILLUSTRATED BY **GREG PIZZOLI**

WHAT'S AN APPLE?

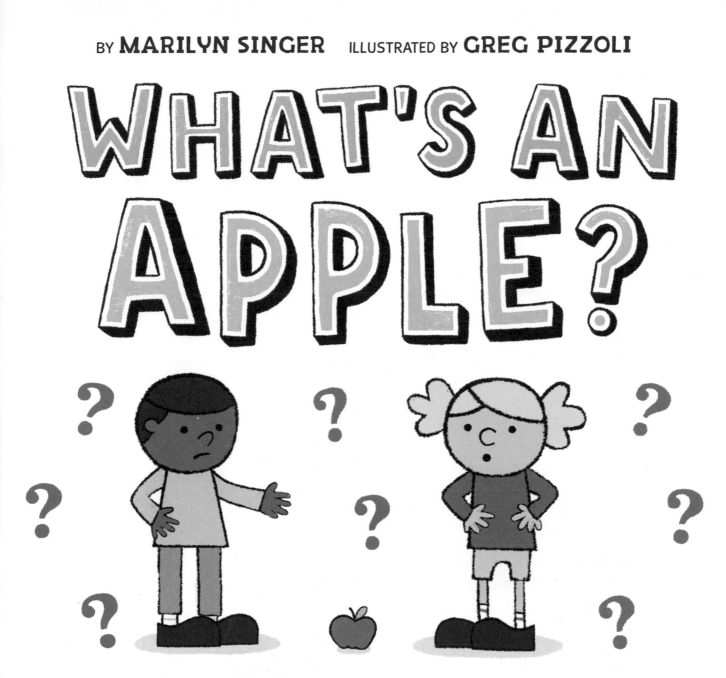

ABRAMS APPLESEED
New York

You can pick it.

You can kick it.

You can throw
away the core.

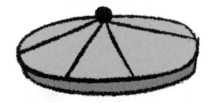

You can toss it.

You can sauce it.

You can roll it on the floor.

You can wash it,

try to squash it,

or pretend that it's a ball.

You can drink it.

You can sink it.

Give your teacher one this fall!

You can snuggle it,

or juggle it,

or put it in a pile.

You can bob for it.

Don't sob for it—

a slice will make you smile.

You can peel it.

Do not steal it!

Use it in a relay race.

You can smell it,

caramel it.

You can eat it anyplace.

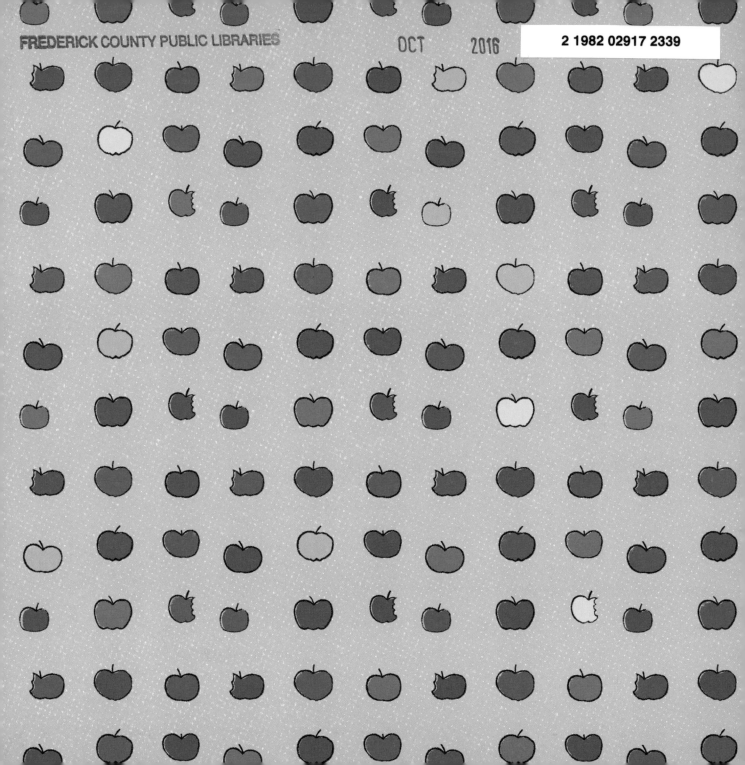